Alan

First published in 2018 in Great Britain by
Barrington Stoke Ltd
18 Walker Street, Edinburgh, EH3 7LP

www.barringtonstoke.co.uk

Text © 2018 Alan Gibbons
Illustrations © 2018 Chris Chalik

A CIP catalogue record for this book is available
from the British Library upon request

ISBN: 978-1-78112-771-1

Printed in China by Leo

Contents

Chapter 1
No "i" in defeat

Red Star 4–East End United 1

Cairo kicked his water bottle down the touchline. His eyes were hard and angry.

Ayo picked up the bottle and handed it back. "Calm down," he said.

Cairo gave Ayo his best dead-eyed look.

"What if I don't want to calm down?" he snapped. "Nobody's giving me the ball. How am I supposed to score if I don't get the ball?"

"I'm the coach," Ayo told him, "and if you don't stop shouting, I'll have to sub you."

Cairo threw his arms in the air. "You can't do that!" he shouted. "I'm the best player you've got. I'm the captain."

Hamza was their number 5. He looked across at Cairo and shook his head. "There's no 'i' in team," he said.

"Oh yeah?" Cairo said, taking a step forward. "Well, there's no 'i' in butt out either, so butt out, butt face."

Hamza squared up to Cairo. He was bigger than him and his shoulders were wide.

"Who's going to make me?" Hamza said, his voice cold.

Ayo stepped between them before the argument turned into a fight. They were two of his best players, but they both had tempers that caught fire far too fast.

"Just calm it, will you?" Ayo said. "We're only three–one down."

"Only?" Cairo yelled. He turned his fury on Ayo. "Red Star are two places above us in the table. We've got to beat them or we'll fall even further behind."

Some of the boys from Red Star were listening to the argument and they began to laugh.

"Who are you laughing at?" Cairo snarled.

Ayo turned to the Red Star coach. "I'm sorry about this," he said. "I'll sort it."

The Red Star coach just shrugged.

"What are you saying sorry to him for?" Cairo demanded.

"Because," Ayo said, "you are letting yourself down."

"Ayo's right," John-Joe said. "Stop throwing a wobbly. We need to sort ourselves out before the second half starts."

At last, Cairo started to listen. John-Joe was his best mate. Ayo smiled and the boys gathered round him.

"Listen," Ayo said, "you played some good stuff, but you're not working together as a team."

Hamza gave Cairo a look.

Cairo ignored him and stared hard at Ayo. "I've scored most of our goals this season," he said. "You need to get me on the ball."

Hamza went to say something, but Ayo frowned. It was his way of telling Hamza it would only start another fight. He turned back to face Cairo.

"Cairo," Ayo said. "You can't just hang around up front waiting for the ball to come to you. Red Star's midfield is working really hard. Our lads are under pressure. You need to come back a bit and help them out."

"But I'm a striker," Cairo moaned. He twisted round to point to the number 9 on his shirt. "How can I score if I'm back in midfield?"

Ayo took Cairo to one side.

"Will you listen to me," he said. "I don't mean stay there all the time. Just drop back when Red Star are all over us like a rash. Give us an outlet. If all we do is hammer it forward, Red Star will keep coming back at us. Can you give it a go?"

Cairo looked down at the grass. "Maybe."

And so, when the second half kicked off, Cairo dropped back a couple of times and put in a few tackles. But he wanted to be up front. He hated defence. He hated midfield. His heart wasn't in it. He saw Ayo on the touchline, trying to catch his eye, but he looked away. At last, John-Joe picked up the ball and got away from the Red Star midfield players.

Cairo made his run. "Pass. Pass!"

Cairo was in the area with his arm up.

"John-Joe. Pass!" he yelled.

Before John-Joe could put his foot through the ball, one of the Red Star boys flicked the ball away. United's chance had gone. Cairo ran after John-Joe.

"You've got to pass it faster," he shouted. "Didn't you hear me?"

Hamza was walking past. "Everybody heard you," he said.

"What's that supposed to mean?" Cairo said.

"Work it out for yourself," Hamza said.

That was the last chance the boys got. Red Star scored again five minutes later.

Red Star four. East End United one.

United trooped off the pitch with their heads down.

"I need the ball to score," Cairo said again.

"Zip it, will you," Hamza said.

The boys squared up again.

"Stop," Ayo said. "Just stop." He got the boys to sit down. "Look," he said, "we lost a game. The season isn't over. But it's time you learned some lessons."

"Like what?" John-Joe asked, as he joined them.

Ayo looked at each player in turn.

"OK," he said. "I tried telling you what to do. Maybe you need to find out for yourselves."

"How do you mean?" Hamza asked.

"Who are your favourite players?" Ayo asked.

"Messi," Cairo said. "Ronaldo."

"Pogba," Hamza said. "Kanté."

John-Joe added some more. "Suárez, Sánchez, Ibrahimović."

"There are plenty of good names there," Ayo said, "but they are all modern. Find out about the history of the beautiful game. Learn about players from the past."

"How do we do that?" Cairo asked.

"Try the library," Ayo told him.

"Library?" Cairo snorted. "What are we, geeks?"

The other boys laughed. Ayo smiled.

"Let's talk about it at the next training session."

TODAY'S STARS

Many people think that **Cristiano Ronaldo** and **Lionel Messi** are the world's best footballers. When **Ronaldo** signed for Manchester United in 2003, he was the most expensive teenage footballer ever. He fulfilled his promise ... and more. Fast, strong and with an amazing range of skills, Ronaldo is also a great header of the ball.

He won the Premier League three times with Manchester United. He won the Champions League, FA Cup and FIFA Club World Cup.

With Real Madrid, Ronaldo went on to win La Liga, the Copa Del Rey three times, the Champions League twice and the FIFA Club World Cup Twice.

With his country, Portugal, Ronaldo won the UEFA European Championship.

Lionel Messi is Ronaldo's rival for the title of world's greatest player. He plays for Real Madrid's bitter rivals, FC Barcelona. Messi, like Ronaldo, comes from a working-class background. When he was a

child, Messi had a condition which meant he grew more slowly than other kids. Maybe that's why as a player, he hugs the ground and the ball, and goes off on weaving runs, skipping over tackles. Messi scores with his feet and his head.

With FC Barcelona Messi has won La Liga an astonishing eight times, the Copa Del Rey four times, the UEFA Champions League four times and the FIFA Club World Cup three times.

With his international team, Argentina, Messi has won the FIFA Under-20 World Cup and an Olympic Gold Medal.

Eden Hazard is one of the most exciting players in the world. He comes from a footballing family in Belgium and plays as an attacking midfielder or winger. Many people think he could one day become the best player in the world.

With his club, Chelsea, Hazard has won the Premier League, the Football League Cup and the FIFA Europa League.

Zlatan Ibrahimović is one of the world's best strikers. Tall, strong, powerful and skilful, Ibrahimović has won titles with many clubs. He is from Sweden, but has won the Dutch League twice with Ajax, then the Italian Serie A three times with Inter Milan and one other time with AC Milan. Ibrahimović has also won the Spanish League with FC Barcelona, and the French League four times with Paris Saint-Germain.

In his first season with Manchester United, Ibrahimović won the Football League Cup. Ibrahimović was injured at the time, but the team also won the Europa League.

Manuel Neuer is thought by most to be the greatest goalkeeper of our time. (His only rival is David De Gea.) Neuer is tall and powerful and has great reflexes. He passes the ball brilliantly to outfield players.

With Bayern Munich, Neuer has won the Bundesliga four times. He has won the UEFA Champions League and the FIFA Club World Cup. Neuer has also won the FIFA World Cup with Germany.

Chapter 2
Foul, Ref!

<u>East End United 2–Riverside 3</u>

Ayo was giving his team talk.

"So did you do what I said?" he asked.

"Sure," Cairo said, with a grin. "Whatever."

"So you found out what makes good teams tick?"

Cairo and John-Joe were laughing. Hamza joined in. They were friends again.

"Yes, we all went down to the library. We read all the books."

They cracked up. Ayo planted his hands on his hips.

"So what did you learn?" he asked.

Cairo was the one who answered.

"Reading hurts your eyes," he said. "Books smell real bad."

Now everybody laughed.

"You didn't go, did you?"

"No," they said.

"Boys," Ayo said. "You're killing me. Off you go. And don't forget to play for each other, not yourselves."

They had their team mate, Tomasz back in goal. He had been visiting family in Poland when they lost last week.

"We're going to keep a clean sheet, Tom," Cairo told him.

Tomasz clapped his strong hands together. His goalie gloves made them look even bigger.

"No problem," Tomasz said with a laugh.

The United players were super confident today. Sure, they'd lost to Red Star last week, but Red Star was a top team. Riverside wasn't. They were near the bottom of the table.

"Get the ball forward," Cairo said to the rest of his team. "I'll do the rest."

He was as good as his word. After five minutes, Hamza won the ball on the halfway line and looked up. Cairo was making a run. Hamza nodded and looped the ball over the top.

Cairo ran onto it and slotted the ball under the keeper's body.

One–nil.

"Easy peasy." Cairo chuckled.

"Lemon squeezy," Hamza said, with a fist-bump to his mate's arm.

After that, United were knocking the ball around, forcing Riverside back. It took desperate defending to keep them out. Cairo hit the bar and had another shot scrambled off the goal line.

"Keep the pressure on," Cairo said. "This could be a cricket score."

Ayo was shouting something from the touchline, but nobody was listening. They were having too much fun. Then United got their second goal. Cairo beat his man and crossed the ball to the far post. John-Joe ran in and headed it home. Two–nil and United were coasting. But Ayo was still trying to get their attention.

"What's up with him?" Cairo asked.

"He says we're committing too many players forward," Hamza said. "We could get caught on the counter-attack."

Cairo shook his head. "We're two–nil up," he said. "What more does he want?"

Just before half-time, Cairo was showboating, doing step-overs on the edge of the Riverside box.

"Pass it," Hamza shouted. "Pass."

Cairo decided to go it alone, but he lost the ball.

"Foul, ref!" he yelled.

The ref played on. Riverside were on the attack now and United only had one defender back. Cairo dived into the tackle, but the Riverside players did a one-two and left him on his backside.

"Come out!" John-Joe yelled.

Tomasz tried to make his body fill the goal, but he had three players bearing down on him. They passed round him.

Two–one.

Cairo was running after the referee.

"Ref, ref!" he yelled. "That was a foul. That lad kicked my ankle."

The ref ignored him.

"It was a foul. No goal."

Now, at last, the ref looked at Cairo.

"The goal stands," she said. "Play on."

Cairo held out his hands, looking for support. Hamza shook his head.

"What's that supposed to mean?" Cairo demanded.

"You lost the ball," Hamza said. "You were being selfish."

They glared at each other, just like last week. Two minutes later, the whistle blew for half-time.

"OK, boys," Ayo said. "You started well, but you lost your discipline towards the end of the half."

"That was Cairo showboating," Hamza grumbled.

"I was fouled!" Cairo yelled, hot with anger.

21

"You kicked your own foot," Hamza said. "Donkey."

He did a clumsy little dance to show how stupid Cairo looked. Cairo glared.

"Calm down," Ayo said. "You're still a goal in front. Just don't leave the back door open."

"What does that mean?" John-Joe asked.

"You've got to defend as well," Ayo said. "You can't just charge after the ball in attack."

The boys nodded, but as soon as they won a corner at the start of the second half, they forgot all about defence. It took a brilliant save to keep Hamza out. United were pressing again then John-Joe slipped and Riverside went on the counter-attack. Once again, Tomasz was left alone to defend his goal.

Two–all.

"That's your fault," Hamza shouted at John-Joe.

"I slipped," John-Joe protested. "I didn't do it on purpose."

"Yeah, leave him alone," Cairo said.

They were still squabbling when Riverside got the ball again and swept down the pitch. The Riverside striker went down under a challenge. The ref blew for a penalty.

"Dive," Cairo protested. "He dived."

The ref went over to Ayo.

"Talk to your player, coach," she said, "Or he's going to get himself in trouble."

Ayo nodded.

"Don't worry. He's coming off."

Cairo was about to protest, but he saw the look in Ayo's eyes. He had to watch while his team went down to a three–two defeat.

"We never lose two on the bounce," Cairo complained.

"I know," John-Joe said. "Maybe we should go to the library after all, see what it is Ayo wants us to learn."

BAD BOYS

The best players sometimes have the worst tempers.
Here are a few of football's hot-heads.

Zinedine Zidane was FIFA World Player of the Year
three times. Born in Marseille, Zidane was one of
the world's most thrilling players. He won Serie A
twice with Juventus before winning La Liga with Real
Madrid. He also won the UEFA Champions League
with Real. In 1998, he won the FIFA World Cup with
the French team and was also awarded the Légion
d'honneur.

Zidane's most famous "bad boy" moment came in
the 2006 World Cup final. Before the game in Berlin
he was awarded the Golden Ball as the best player
in the tournament. Seven minutes into the game,
he put France in the lead with a penalty. Marco
Materazzi equalised for Italy and the match went
into extra time. Materazzi insulted Zidane and
Zidane head-butted him in the chest. Italy won the
final on penalties.

There is a statue of this famous head-butt in Doha, Qatar. It is said to celebrate a moment not of victory, but of defeat.

Along with **Pelé**, **Diego Maradona** is one of the greatest footballing geniuses ever, but he may be best known for breaking the rules. Like Messi, Maradona isn't tall, but he was an amazingly skilful and tricky player. He won the Argentinian premier league with Boca Juniors and Serie A twice with Napoli. With his country, Argentina, he won the World Cup once and came runner-up once.

However, perhaps his most famous moment is the "Hand of God" in the World Cup against England when Maradona guided the ball into the net with his hand for the first goal. He said it was God helping him out! He later dribbled through the England defence to score a brilliant winner with his feet.

Eric Cantona was a superb French player. He won the French first division twice with Marseille and helped Leeds to the old First Division championship.

He then moved to Manchester United, where he won the Premier League four times and the FA Cup twice.

Cantona is best known for the moment in 1995 when he jumped into the crowd at Crystal Palace to kung-fu kick a fan who had insulted him. He was banned from playing for eight months.

Not many goalkeepers are seen as bad boys, but **Harald "Toni" Schumacher** of West Germany earned himself the title. He played 76 times for his national side. He also won the Bundesliga with FC Köln and Borussia Dortmund and the Turkish championship with Fenerbahçe S.K.

In the 1982 World Cup semi-final France's Patrick Battiston and Schumacher went for the same ball. Battiston got there first, but Schumacher jumped in the air and crashed into the French player. The impact was so great that Battiston lost two teeth and had three cracked ribs.

But West Germany lost 3–1 in the final to Italy.

Chapter 3
That's teamwork

The plan to read about the great players of the past was almost over before it had begun. While Hamza, John-Joe and Tomasz looked up at the building with frowns on their faces, Cairo went to read the notice on the big wooden door.

"*Library shut,*" he read. "*Your nearest library is now Central Library.* Shut? Why's it shut? That sucks."

"No matter," Hamza said. "We've got plenty of time and we can get the bus there."

"We'd better do it," John-Joe said. "Ayo will keep going on about it until we do."

Everybody shrugged.

"Why have they shut the local library anyway?" Tomasz said. "That's proper stupid."

Cairo shook his head. "Money, I suppose."

When they got off the bus, they kicked an old cardboard box down the street as they made their way to the library. It was a huge building on four floors. Everybody seemed to know where they were going except them.

"OK," Hamza said, "where do we start?"

A woman came over. She was wearing a badge that said *Here to Help*.

"What are you looking for, boys?" she asked.

They told her and the librarian helped them find as many football books as she could.

Soon, they were relaxing on beanbags or lying on the floor, flicking through the pages. Cairo got onto one of the PCs and looked for more information.

"Come and see this guy," Cairo said. "He is one of the greats, Pelé."

He had found a clip from the 1970 World Cup, Brazil against Italy. In it, Pelé takes one, two, three touches. The great man is in control of the ball. He is like an army colonel. He waits, waits for the right time. He is in no rush.

"See how he looks for the run," Cairo said, his voice excited.

Pelé is going to play it into space. None of the defenders even see who he is passing to. Then, out of the blue, Brazil captain Carlos Alberto makes a diagonal run into the box. Pelé rolls the ball. The pass is perfect. It takes a bobble, but Carlos Alberto strikes it with his right foot into the far corner.

"Goal!" Cairo cried. "Sweet as a nut!"

A few people turned round.

"Isn't somebody supposed to say *shush*?" Hamza asked.

"I think that's a bit old-fashioned now." John-Joe chuckled. "Lots of people are talking."

"Yeah, but they're not shouting," Tomasz said.

The boys didn't just look at the flair players. They looked at the organisers, men like Bobby Moore, who was captain of England when they won the World Cup, and German captain Franz "Der Kaiser" Beckenbauer.

"Maybe we need a captain like that," Hamza said.

"We've already got a captain," Cairo said. "Me. We don't need no Kaiser –"

John-Joe sighed. "Don't you two start fighting again."

The librarian showed them how to join the library and they set off home. When they got off the bus they saw some boys they knew playing football.

"Fancy a game?" Hamza said. "Four a side."

The other boys nodded. It was one all when Cairo barged his own player off the ball. Hamza got up off the ground.

"I would have scored then," he snapped, angry about the push. "You're being greedy as usual."

"I'm the captain," Cairo told him. "I call the shots."

"No you don't," Hamza protested. "That's not what a captain does."

John-Joe stepped between them.

"Cut it out," he told them. "Look, Cairo, you're my best mate, but Hamza's right. He had a good chance and you robbed your own player. That's just wrong."

Cairo's jaw dropped, but he didn't say anything else. Next time he got the ball, he remembered Pelé and waited for Hamza to race past him. He rolled the ball to his right and Hamza scored.

"See," John-Joe said, "that's teamwork."

On the way home, Tomasz put his arm round Cairo's shoulders.

"Remember Bobby Moore and Franz Beckenbauer," he said. "They were the guys with cool heads. You're our best player, but you're not the best captain. You get angry far too easily."

"Well, who should be captain then?" Cairo asked. "If not me?"

Tomasz turned his head and Cairo saw he was looking at John-Joe.

"John-Joe?" Cairo said. "Really?"

"Everybody likes him," Tomasz said. "He's calm and doesn't always have flies up his nose."

Cairo grinned. "Not like me, you mean."

Tomasz laughed. "You said it."

"And you might just be right," Cairo said. "Let's talk to Ayo about it."

FLAIR PLAYERS

We talked about **Diego Maradona** in Bad Boys. Most people think Maradona's greatest rival was the best player ever. He lives in Brazil and his name is ...

Edson Arantes do Nascimento or **Pelé**. He scored 1,281 goals in 1,363 games. With the Brazilian club Santos, he won the country's Serie A six times. With Brazil, he won the FIFA World Cup three times. But Pelé was not just a brilliant goal scorer, he was also a hard-working member of the team. Later in his career, he dropped deep, playing as an attacking midfielder. What people love about Pelé is the joy with which he played – a style known as "samba football", like the dance that comes from Brazil too. Many fans think the 1970 World Cup-winning Brazil side was a true "dream team" – the greatest side ever.

When people use the term "Total Football", they often think of the Dutch national team and its greatest player, **Johan Cruyff**. In Total Football, no player plays a fixed part. If one player changes position, a team mate fills in. Cruyff won the Dutch league eight times with Ajax and once with Feyenoord. He also won the European Cup three times with Ajax. As a manager, Cruyff won the Dutch league and the UEFA Cup Winners' Cup with Ajax. With Barcelona, he won La Liga four times, the Champions League and the Cup Winners' Cup.

Chapter 4
When the going gets tough

Junior Lions 2–East End United 3

When they met for training that evening, Ayo asked what they'd learned.

"You need the best footballers," Cairo said, still buzzing after the visit to the library. "You need ball players like Pelé, Maradona, Cruyff. You need guys like Puskás and Di Stéfano."

"You've got some great names there," Ayo said. "Who's your favourite?"

Cairo thought for a moment.

"It's got to be Pelé," he said.

"OK," Ayo said. "Why?"

Hamza laughed. "Easy. Cairo thinks he's as good as Pelé."

"Shut up, you," Cairo said, only half joking. "No, the Brazil team has this style, the 'ginga'. It's the soul of football. It means playing full of joy, like dancing. Pele was the King of Ginga."

Tomasz put his hand up. "You need flair and style, true," he said, "but there's no point scoring three and letting in four."

"I agree with Tomasz," Hamza said. "We're not tight enough. We're way behind the two top teams. We lose any more games and we're stuffed."

Ayo looked around. "So what are you saying?"

Tomasz looked at Cairo. "We need a new captain," he said, "a defender or midfielder, somebody who will get us organised from the back."

"Too right," Hamza said, as he gave Cairo a playful nudge in the ribs. "This guy here is more skilful than any of us, but he shouts way too much."

Cairo grinned. "You got me there."

"So who are we talking about?" Ayo asked.

Tomasz pointed. "We want John-Joe."

"Does everybody agree?" Ayo asked, with a smile.

Everyone nodded, even Cairo.

"OK," Ayo said. "Let's talk about Sunday. We're up against the Junior Lions, the best team after Red Star. If we win this one, we put ourselves back up there, near the top of the league."

"It won't be easy," John-Joe said. "We played them on the first day of the season. They beat us four–nil."

"Yes," Hamza said, "and it could have been worse."

"So, what did we do wrong then?" Ayo asked.

Cairo made a joke. "You didn't give me the ball."

Everybody pelted him with their paper cups. When they had all stopped laughing, John-Joe had his say.

"All we did was try to score," he said. "When we lost possession, the Junior Lions ran down the other end and scored. We've got to attack as a team, but we've also got to defend as a team."

Ayo clapped his hands. "OK," he said. "Let's have everyone on this side in their bibs. Everyone on this side, no bibs. Let's try out some ideas."

*

The following Sunday it was wet. The ball zipped off the surface of the pitch.

"Don't hit the ball too hard," John-Joe said. "It will run out of play."

The Junior Lions looked cocky. They all remembered their easy win on the first day of the season but, in the first five minutes of this match, they found out that United were no push-over. John-Joe won the ball halfway inside his own half and rolled it to Hamza. Hamza hit a sweet ball for Cairo and Cairo struck it hard against the crossbar.

"Close," Tomasz shouted from his goal line.

That woke the Juniors up. They went on the attack and pinned United down in their own half. Then they took the lead after fifteen minutes.

"I don't get it," Cairo said. "It's happening all over again."

"Keep your head up," John-Joe said. "You don't sort things right away. Keep playing. We'll nail it soon."

Cairo wasn't so sure. The Juniors scored with a header just before half-time and nearly made it three. He saw how glad the United players were to hear the whistle go for half-time.

"So, where's it going wrong?" Ayo asked. "Any ideas?"

"Don't look at me," Cairo said, confused. "I'm not being greedy this time."

"No," Hamza said. "You've only had one shot."

"I think that what John-Joe said before is right," Hamza chipped in. "In this game, first we're all attack then we're all defence."

Tomasz agreed. "I've had to make too many saves. The ball keeps coming back at me. I tell you, my legs are like jelly."

Ayo smiled. "You're getting there, lads," he said. "Keep it solid at the back, but move it forward faster and give our front men more possession, too. It's not just Cairo that's in front, either. Don't forget T.J. here."

T.J. was the youngest kid in the team. He was a striker, and had a good eye for the goal, but he was a bit short and skinny. Defenders had no problem bullying him off the ball.

"You're a strong lad, Cairo," Ayo said. "You need to give T.J. some protection."

Ten minutes into the second half, two Juniors players doubled up on T.J. Cairo joined in the scrum for the ball and T.J. came away with it. He turned left, turned right, dropped his shoulder and swept the ball into the net. It all happened in the blink of an eye.

"Yes!" Cairo yelled, lifting T.J. off his feet. "We're back in the game."

All of a sudden, the confidence was flowing and the boys played with flair.

The Junior Lions were dropping deeper and United were enjoying their football. Hamza wasn't needed in defence, so he burst through the middle, laid off the ball to T.J. and took the return. He looked up and saw Cairo as he stormed into the box. Hamza flighted a pass and it bounced off Cairo's knee into the net.

"You need a bit of luck," Cairo said with a laugh.

But after that, it was all Juniors. They were chasing a winning goal to break the deadlock. Everybody was back, even Cairo.

"We need Cairo to defend," John-Joe said. "He's tall and strong. But we need an outlet up front too. T.J., you stay up."

Hamza watched T.J. race off.

"He's flying," he said. "I didn't know he was that fast."

After that, Tomasz tipped one shot onto the post and Hamza cleared off the line. Cairo picked up the ball and saw T.J. scampering forward. He hit it high over the Juniors defence. T.J. ran fast onto it and clipped the ball home.

"Nice one!" Ayo said, with a fist-bump for every player as he came off. "We attacked as a team. We defended as a team. When the going got tough, we had a leader. You know what we are, boys? We're a team."

United were back in the title race.

Game on!

LEADERS ON THE PITCH

Bobby Moore was captain of England in 1966 and led the country to its only win in a World Cup final. Geoff Hurst, who scored a hat-trick in the final, said of Bobby Moore, "He was not a ranter or a raver or a fist-pumping captain." Moore was the youngest England captain ever. He was given the armband at just 22 years old. Pelé said Moore was his greatest opponent in Brazil's one–nil victory over England in the 1970 World Cup, which Brazil went on to win. With his club, West Ham United, Moore also won the FA Cup and the Cup Winners' Cup the following year.

Franz Beckenbauer won every football trophy going. His nickname was "Der Kaiser", which means "the Emperor" in German. Beckenbauer played the 1970 World Cup with a dislocated shoulder. He led West Germany to victory in Euro 1972 and in the 1974 World Cup final and won five Bundesliga titles, four DFB-Pokals, three European Cups, one Cup Winners' Cup and one Intercontinental Cup at club level. As a manager, he won the World Cup with Germany and the Bundesliga and UEFA Cup with Bayern Munich.

Francisco Gento is the most successful club captain of all time. The Spanish player won twelve La Liga trophies, six European Cups, two Copa del Rey, two Latin Cups and one Intercontinental Cup with Real Madrid, the club which he served from the age of 20 to 38.

Paolo Maldini was captain of A.C. Milan for twelve years and the Italy national side for eight. His nickname was "Il Capitano". With Milan, he won the Champions League five times, seven Serie A titles, five Supercoppe Italiane, five European Super Cups, two Intercontinental Cups, one Coppa Italia and one FIFA Club World Cup title. He said that his greatest disappointment was that he reached the World Cup final twice with Italy, but never won the trophy.

Chapter 5
All or nothing

East End United 3–Red Star 2

The maths was simple. East End United were two points behind Red Star at the top of the table. The final game of the season saw the two top teams face each other, which meant that United had to win. Any other result gave the league title to Red Star.

"Squeaky bottom time," Cairo said.

Nobody laughed. Not even a flicker of a smile. The whole team was tense.

"Come on, lads," Cairo said. "Say something."

"They beat us four–one last time," Hamza said. "Doesn't that bother you?"

"No way," Cairo said. "We were a different team then."

"We're not that different," T.J. said. "We're the same bunch of players."

"We're the same, only different," John-Joe grunted.

Cairo shook his head. "What's that supposed to mean?"

It was Ayo's turn to speak.

"I think what John-Joe is trying to say is that you're the same guys, but at last you're playing as a team," Ayo told them. "You're playing for one another."

Tomasz looked across at the Red Star team. "They're still a really good team," he said.

John-Joe got to his feet. "Then we've got to be better. Last time, we were three–one down by half-time. They'll try to do the same again, win the game early on. We keep it tight and stay in touch. We'll get our chances, take our luck."

The boys nodded, but everyone was down in the dumps. The pressure was almost too much.

United kicked off, but the ball ran away from T.J. and Red Star came on strong. It was attack after attack. Cairo had to drop back and help protect his defence. After 15 minutes, Red Star had their best shot on goal, but Tomasz clawed it away for a corner and Cairo headed it off the line.

"Great header," John-Joe said.

But there was a problem. With Cairo more in defence, T.J. was on his own up front. He had two defenders marking him and he couldn't get a sniff of the ball.

"I need to help him out," Cairo said as he gazed down at the other end of the pitch.

"Not yet," John-Joe told him. "We need you back here."

Then, just before half-time, Hamza made a mistake and gifted the ball to Red Star. Then they were one–nil down.

"What do you call that?" Cairo shouted. "You do know what side you're on, don't you?"

Hamza's face turned to thunder, but John-Joe stepped in.

"Look," he said, "it was a mistake. No need to yell at each other."

"Well, I'm going up front," Cairo snapped. "T.J needs me and we need to equalise."

"Not yet," John-Joe told him. "We can't afford to give another goal away."

"You're wrong," Cairo said, as angry as Hamza now. "We can't just defend."

"This is Red Star," John-Joe said. "They've got their tails up. We have to keep them out."

Tomasz came over from his goal.

"He's right, Cairo," he said, "and he's the captain."

Cairo stamped away, but he kept on with his job in defence and cleared another shot off the line before half-time.

"This sucks," he said as they gathered round Ayo at half-time.

"We're in a better position than we were last time," Ayo said. "Keep it tight from now on and we'll see how things go."

"Then we'll commit more men forward?" Cairo asked.

"Yes."

*

Ten minutes into the second half, and United had only had one scare. Tomasz had pushed a brutal shot against the post, but it was still one–nil. John-Joe looked across at Ayo and got the nod.

"OK, Cairo," he said. "Red Star are tiring."

"About time," Hamza said.

Cairo trotted forward to join T.J. And, all of a sudden, it was a different game, a lot more even. Both sides had chances then Tomasz got the ball and belted it down field, fast and accurate. It fell into the path of T.J. He left his marker for dead and powered down the touchline before crossing the ball in. Cairo hurled his body at the ball and headed it past the keeper.

One–one.

United were back in the game.

"We're going to win this," Cairo said.

"We've still got a lot of work to do," John-Joe said.

It was end-to-end stuff. Now the two teams were evenly matched and they both had chances. With ten minutes to go, T.J. got the ball and raced into the area, his feet flying over the grass. The big Red Star centre-back took him down.

"Penalty!" The ref pointed to the spot.

Cairo's heart was banging. He put the ball on the spot, took a short run up and hammered it into the top right-hand corner.

"Goal!"

It was two–one. If the score stayed that way, the title belonged to United.

Cairo winked at the rest of his team.

"They think it's all over," he said. "It is now."

"Don't talk too soon," John-Joe said with a frown. "Keep your focus. They could still equalise."

But this time, it wasn't Cairo who got them into trouble with his showboating. With five minutes to go, John-Joe tried a step-over and stumbled. The Red Star striker jumped on the ball and scored with a screamer of a shot.

Two all.

Now Red Star were back in the driving seat.

"Sorry," John-Joe muttered, as his eyes
stung with tears. "I'm so sorry."

Cairo saw his friend's head drop and went
over. They had less than five minutes to go.
But to everybody's surprise, Cairo wasn't angry.

"Come on, John-Joe, we can still do this,"
Cairo said, his voice soft. "First chance you get,
give me the ball."

John-Joe still looked upset, but he nodded.
The next few minutes were frustrating. Every
Red Star player was back in defence and United
couldn't create any chances.

Cairo came hunting for the ball in midfield.
Then John-Joe won a sliding tackle. Hamza
picked up the loose ball and flicked it to Cairo.
Cairo went on a heart-bursting run down the

pitch. Nobody could live with his pace. T.J. peeled away, yelling for the ball. His run attracted two Red Star defenders and that was just what Cairo needed. His lungs were on fire, but this was his last chance to win it for his team. He burst into the area. The Red Star keeper rushed out.

"Shoot!" Tomasz yelled from his line. "SHOOT!"

In that moment, the world seemed to move in slow motion. It was a lousy angle and Cairo knew that if he shot the keeper would block it. His only hope was to try something amazing. And so he played by instinct and flicked the ball up and over the keeper with the outside of his boot. It floated past the goalie's gloves and into the net.

Cairo wheeled away, arms in the air and set off on a run down the line. Moments before, he'd been dead on his feet. Now he was on

fire with fresh energy. He found Hamza and Tomasz and they fell in a heap.

"One minute to go," John-Joe said. "Calm down, lads. No mistakes."

United won the ball from the kick-off. Hamza passed it to Cairo. Normally, Cairo would have headed for goal. This time, he did the opposite. He took it into the corner and blocked the defenders. They were kicking at his legs, trying to get the ball. He didn't kick back, didn't protest. He took one for the team.

Moments later, the whistle blew.

Three–two.

United were champions.

"We did it," Cairo said. "Teamwork won it for us."

"Yes," John-Joe said, "teamwork was part of it, but Red Star matched us man for man. They were as good as us except for one thing. We had a special player who made the difference."

Cairo thought his heart was going to burst, this time with pride. Then the day got even better. He saw Ayo coming over. Mum and Dad were with him. Then there was a guy he didn't know. Ayo introduced him – he was a scout for one of the big clubs.

"Mr Harris liked what he saw," Ayo said. "He wants to talk with you and your parents."

Cairo stared at him. Was this for real?

"Can I share this moment with the team first?" he asked.

"Knock yourself out," Ayo said, with a wide grin.

As Cairo jogged away, he heard Ayo add something.

"That's what makes him so good," he told Mr Harris. "He's got skill and flair, but he's a proper team player too."

John-Joe joined in with Cairo as he headed for the rest of the United team ...

"It took a bit of time," he said, as he slapped Cairo on the back. "But you got there in the end."

Our books are tested
for children and young people by
children and young people.

Thanks to everyone who consulted on
a manuscript for their time and effort in
helping us to make our books better
for our readers.